www.korkypaul.com

Endpapers by Oska Paul aged 7 1/4

For Sharon and Martin, who are always full of good ideas V.T.
For Ron Heapy K.P.

OXFORD
UNIVERSITY PRESS

Great Clarendon Street, Oxford OX2 6DP

Oxford University Press is a department of the University of Oxford.
It furthers the University's objective of excellence in research, scholarship,
and education by publishing worldwide in

Oxford New York

Athens Auckland Bangkok Bogotá Buenos Aires Calcutta
Cape Town Chennai Dar es Salaam Delhi Florence Hong Kong Istanbul
Karachi Kuala Lumpur Madrid Melbourne Mexico City Mumbai
Nairobi Paris São Paulo Singapore Taipei Tokyo Toronto Warsaw

with associated companies in Berlin Ibadan

Oxford is a registered trade mark of Oxford University Press
in the UK and in certain other countries

British Library Cataloguing in Publication Data available

ISBN 0-19-272348-0 (paperback)
     0-19-279026-9 (hardback)

Printed in Portugal

Korky Paul and Valerie Thomas

Winnie Flies Again

OXFORD
UNIVERSITY PRESS

Winnie the Witch always travelled by broomstick.
It was a wonderful way to travel.

Winnie would jump onto her broomstick.
Wilbur would jump onto her shoulder.
And they would zoom up into the sky.

There were no traffic lights.
No traffic jams.

Just the empty sky.

Well, that was how it used to be.
But, just lately, the sky had become
rather crowded.

Last week, Winnie didn't see a helicopter.
Wilbur lost two of his whiskers.

The week before that, she didn't see a hang glider.

Wilbur's tail was bent.

The week before that, a very tall building suddenly got in her way.

Wilbur lost a clump of fur.

'The sky is too dangerous, Wilbur,' said Winnie.
'We'll have to try something else.'
So she took out her wand, waved it, and shouted

ABRACADABRA!

Her broomstick turned into a bicycle.
But it was very slow.
Very hard to pedal.

And then a pond got in Winnie's way.
'She should look where she's going,' croaked a frog.

'A bicycle is worse than a broomstick, Wilbur,' said Winnie.
'We'll have to try something else.'
So she took out her wand, waved it, and shouted

ABRACADABRA!

Her bicycle turned into a skateboard.
The skateboard was fast.
But it was hard to steer.
And impossible to stop.

Winnie was stopped. By an ice-cream seller.
'Can't you see where you're going?' he shouted.

'A skateboard is worse than a bicycle, Wilbur,' said Winnie.
'We'll have to try something else.'
So she took out her wand, waved it, and shouted

ABRACADABRA!

Her skateboard turned into a horse,
and they trotted slowly down the path.
'This is much better than bicycles or skateboards,'
said Winnie.

But she didn't see . . .

. . . the low branch of a tree.
This time, Winnie didn't say anything.
She was hanging from a branch.

Slowly and carefully, Winnie climbed down from the tree.

'I think we'll walk home, Wilbur,' said Winnie.

They limped slowly along the road.
It was a very very slow way to travel.

But it was safe.

DANGER

Until Winnie stepped into a hole
and tumbled deep down under the ground.

YES
WE're
OPEN

'I think I need a cup of tea,'
Winnie said.

Winnie climbed out of the tunnel and went into a shop.

'A cup of tea and a muffin, please,' she said.
'And a saucer of milk for my cat.'

'We don't sell cups of tea or muffins,'
said the shop lady.
'And we don't have saucers of milk.
But I think I can help you.'

And she sold Winnie a pair of spectacles.

Now, Winnie and Wilbur travel everywhere by broomstick.
It's a wonderful way to travel.